Note to parents, carers and teachers

Read it yourself is a series of modern stories, favourite characters and traditional tales written in a simple way for children who are learning to read. The books can be read independently or as part of a guided reading session.

Each book is carefully structured to include many high-frequency words vital for first reading. The sentences on each page are supported closely by pictures to help with understanding, and to offer lively details to talk about.

The books are graded into four levels that progressivel introduce wider vocabulary and longer stories as a reader's ability and confidence grows.

Ideas for use

- Begin by looking through the book and talking about the pictures. Has your child heard this story before?

- Help your child with any words he does not know, either by helping him to sound them out or supplying them yourself.

- Developing readers can be concentrating so hard on the words that they sometimes don't fully grasp the meaning of what they're reading. Answering the puzzle questions at the end of the book will help with understanding.

For more information and advice on Read it yourself and book banding, visit www.ladybird.com/readityourself

Book Band 7

Level 2 is ideal for children who have received some reading instruction and can read short, simple sentences with help.

Special features:

Frequent repetition of main story words and phrases

Short, simple sentences

Careful match between story and pictures

Large, clear type

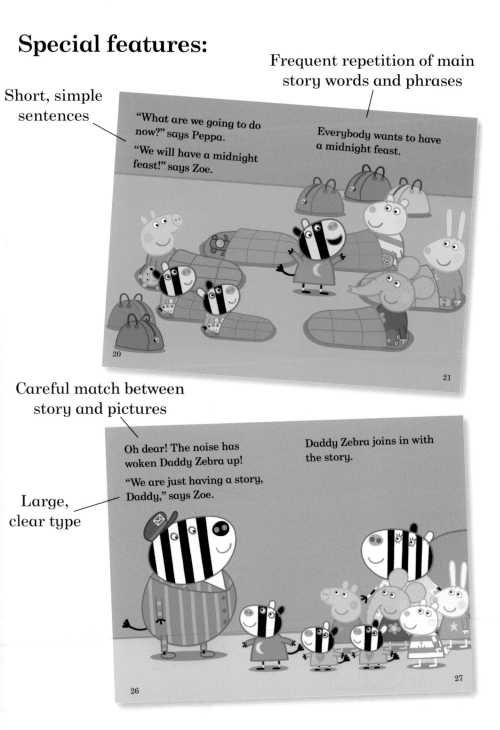

"What are we going to do now?" says Peppa.

"We will have a midnight feast!" says Zoe.

Everybody wants to have a midnight feast.

20

21

Oh dear! The noise has woken Daddy Zebra up!

"We are just having a story, Daddy," says Zoe.

Daddy Zebra joins in with the story.

26

27

Educational Consultant: Geraldine Taylor
Book Banding Consultant: Kate Ruttle

LADYBIRD BOOKS

UK | USA | Canada | Ireland | Australia
India | New Zealand | South Africa

Ladybird Books is part of the Penguin Random House group of companies
whose addresses can be found at global.penguinrandomhouse.com.
www.penguin.co.uk   www.puffin.co.uk   www.ladybird.co.uk

Penguin
Random House
UK

Text adapted from Peppa's First Sleepover, first published 2012
Read It Yourself edition published 2016
This edition published 2018
002

This book copyright © ABD Ltd/Ent. One UK Ltd 2012, 2016

This book is based on the TV series Peppa Pig.
Peppa Pig is created by Neville Astley and Mark Baker.
Peppa Pig © Astley Baker Davies Ltd/Entertainment One UK Ltd 2003.
www.peppapig.com

Printed in China

A CIP catalogue record for this book is available from the British Library

ISBN: 978-0-241-35313-4

All correspondence to:
Ladybird Books
Penguin Random House Children's
8 Viaduct Gardens, London SW11 7BW

MIX
Paper from
responsible sources
FSC® C018179

First Sleepover

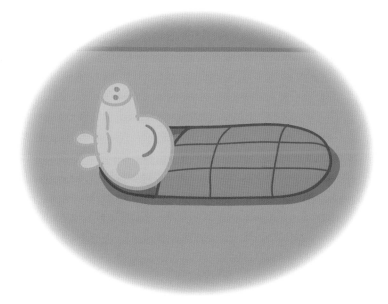

Adaptation written by Ellen Philpott
Based on the TV series *Peppa Pig*. *Peppa Pig* is
created by Neville Astley and Mark Baker

Peppa is going to a sleepover at Zoe Zebra's house.

"Hello, Peppa!" says Zoe.

Rebecca Rabbit, Suzy Sheep
and Emily Elephant are
at Zoe's house, too.

Everybody says hello
to Peppa.

"Be very quiet, girls!" says Mummy Zebra. "Don't wake Daddy Zebra up. He has to go to work in the morning."

"Can we join in with the sleepover?" say Zoe's little sisters.

Zoe does not want them to.

"You are too little," she says.

Oh dear! Zoe's little sisters are crying! They want to be at the sleepover, too.

"Can they join in?" says Rebecca Rabbit.

Zoe says her sisters can join in, so then they stop crying.

"What do you do at a sleepover?" says Suzy.

"We will play a song on the piano," says Zoe.

Emily joins in. Then Peppa joins in.

Everybody plays
on the piano.

Oh dear! Mummy Zebra
has woken up.

"Shh! Stop playing!" says
Mummy Zebra. "Don't wake
Daddy Zebra up! He has to
go to work in the morning."

"What are we going to do now?" says Peppa.

"We will have a midnight feast!" says Zoe.

Everybody wants to have
a midnight feast.

"Shh! Don't make so much noise," says Zoe.

They go and have a midnight feast.

"Be quiet, girls!" says
Mummy Zebra. "Daddy
Zebra has to go to work in
the morning. Just have a
quiet story now."

Everybody joins in with the story. They are not very quiet.

Oh dear! The noise has woken Daddy Zebra up!

"We are just having a story, Daddy," says Zoe.

Daddy Zebra joins in with
the story.

Then Daddy Zebra plays
them a song on the piano.

The quiet song makes
everybody go to sleep!

How much do you remember about the story of Peppa Pig: First Sleepover? Answer these questions and find out!

- Whose house is Peppa going to?

- Which instrument does Zoe play a song on?

- Does Mummy Zebra tell the children to be noisy or quiet?

- Who wants to join in the sleepover?

Look at the pictures and match them to the story words.

Peppa

Suzy Sheep

Emily Elephant

Rebecca Rabbit

Zoe Zebra

www.ladybird.com